STACY

A Novel

By

ARNOLD JACKSON

First Edition
Published in the United States of America
ISBN: 979-8-9996731-1-4 (paperback)
ISBN: 979-8-9996731-2-1 (hardcover)
ISBN: 979-8-9996731-0-7 (ebook)
Cover Design: ARNOLD JACKSON
Interior Design: ARNOLD JACKSON
Printed in the United States of America

Dedication

To the mustard seeds of faith in every soul—tiny rocks that move mountains. And to those who keep moving, even when the stream feels like a dream. In memory of lost loves and awakened hearts.

Epigraph

"He replied, 'Because you have so little faith. Truly I tell you, if you have faith as small as a mustard seed, you can say to this mountain, "Move from here to there," and it will move. Nothing will be impossible for you.'"

— Matthew 17:20 (NIV)

"Such a feelin's comin' over me / There is wonder in most everything I see... / I'm on the top of the world lookin' down on creation / And the only explanation I can find / Is the love that I've found ever since you've been around / Your love's put me at the top of the world."

— "Top of the World" by The Carpenters

Appendix: Esoteric Guide to STACY

(For readers seeking deeper layers: A table decoding names, symbols, and lessons in the esoteric tradition.)

Acknowledgments

Gratitude to the whispers of inspiration—from ancient texts to modern minds—that shaped this tale. To my friend Duncan, who believed in me. To Arthur (My Father) and Elaine (The Grail Bearer) for the spark of creation, and to all who see the hidden crystals in everyday rocks. To my beautiful daughter, Miranda, and my grandson, River.

Introduction

Dear Reader,

Welcome to STACY, a story that unfolds on two planes: the surface narrative of love, loss, invention, and redemption, and a deeper esoteric tapestry woven from threads of neuroscience, spirituality, and myth. At its heart, this is an allegory of the soul's journey—drawing from the pineal gland's calcite microcrystal (a "tiny rock" of enlightenment), the mustard seed of faith (Matthew 17:20; Luke 17:6), and the Lakota legend of the White Buffalo Woman, who brings peace through compassion and transformation.

The tale mirrors embryonic development: Around the seventh week, a calcite crystal forms in the pineal gland (the "third eye"), coinciding with the heart's first beat—symbolizing the soul's incarnation into the physical world. Alen's path reflects this awakening: from grief's shadows to creation's light, battling illusions (material greed, false love) to embrace neuroplasticity as spiritual rewiring. Names and symbols are keys—Alen as the "tiny rock," Stacy as "resurrection," the M1 Beach as the primary motor cortex (first drive into action).

Read it once for the story's emotional arc, a young inventor's fight against corporate theft and personal tragedy. Then revisit with the esoteric lens: Events as soul lessons (Gilgul: reincarnation's refinement), inventions as alchemical tools for healing, and love as the force that moves mountains. The appendix table provides a guide—cross-reference chapters with meanings to unlock hidden depths.

This novel is an invitation to ponder: Is life but a dream, a stream we row gently? Or a seed we nurture into something eternal? May it awaken your own inner crystal.

With faith as small as a mustard seed,
Arnold Jackson
July 23, 2025

STACY
by Arnold Jackson

—-

PROLOGUE

Whispers from the Grave

The wind moved through Oakwood Cemetery like a quiet breath, stirring the cherry blossoms until petals drifted down in slow, pink spirals over the grass.

It was April 1988. Warm. Bright. Almost festive.

And completely wrong.

Alen Bronte stood alone in front of his father's headstone, his hands shoved so deep into the pockets of his denim jacket it looked like he was trying to hold himself together from the inside.

QUINN BRONTE

Beloved Father

1940-1987

The dates were small and polite. The finality behind them was not.

He knelt and brushed a curl of dried leaves off the granite, fingers trailing over his father's name.

"Hey, Dad," he said, and his voice came out thinner than he meant it to. "I, uh... I made it. No parade, though. They don't do that for guys who live above a garage with a corgi and a pile of broken radios."

He tried to laugh. It cracked on the way out.

"Mom's still yelling," he went on quietly. "At the TV. At the mail. At me. Mostly at me. I don't think she knows what to do with... any of this."

He swallowed, tasting the familiar sting behind his eyes.

"I'm trying. I applied to labs, tech places, anywhere with wires and a broken coffee machine. No one's called back." He shrugged. "There's this novelty shop at the mall. Plastic junk, prank gadgets. Not exactly world-changing, but... you always said greatness begins small, right?"

The sun slipped lower, turning the cemetery gold. The names on the stones flared briefly, then faded back to dull gray.

"I keep wondering," Alen said, almost whispering now. "If you'd still be here if I'd built something better. If I'd worked faster. If I'd been smarter."

The breeze moved through the blossoms again. The petals kept falling, indifferent.

"I hope I'm making you proud," he said. "Even a little."

He stayed there until the shadows lengthened and the chill finally seeped through the denim. Then he stood, wiped his eyes with the heel of his hand like a kid who didn't want to be seen crying, and walked back to his car.

On the drive home, the radio crackled to life. Tears for Fears floated through the speakers, the chorus bleeding into the warm evening as the world rolled forward-

whether Alen was ready for it or not.

—-

CHAPTER ONE

Fortunes Folded in Paper

The bell over the door of Wong's Chinese Kitchen jingled in that tired, cheerful way only restaurant bells can manage. Warm air rolled over Alen as he stepped inside, carrying the smell of soy sauce, sesame oil, and something sizzling in garlic.

Fonzie, his corgi, trotted beside him, nails ticking across the tile. The dog's ears perked instantly toward the counter, tail wagging in a hopeful little metronome.

"Back again, Alen?" called Li Aiwen from behind the register. She was small, silver-haired, and had the kind of gaze that saw straight through excuses.

"Back again," he said. "The broccoli beef missed me."

He took his usual corner table, pulled a handful of fortune-cookie papers from his jacket pocket, and went back to folding.

The origami flower was almost done. Each petal was a crease of thin white paper, the tiny blue fortunes tucked inside like secrets:

LOVE BLOOMS WHERE IT IS TENDED.

A SMILE IS A WINDOW TO THE HEART.

YOUR TRUE DESIRE WILL FIND YOU.

He smoothed another crease, tongue caught between his teeth in concentration.

"For Sherri?" Li Aiwen's voice appeared at his elbow.

He jumped. "Jeez, Ms. Li-do you float?"

She chuckled and leaned closer to study the flower. "You don't need fortune cookies," she said. "Your hands tell the story already. This is beautiful. Any woman would treasure it." Her eyes softened. "Sherri is a lucky girl."

"Assuming I don't botch the last petal," he muttered. "This is attempt number three. The others died heroes."

The bell over the door chimed.

Stacy walked in.

She didn't crash into the room; she sort of... arrived. Soft blond hair in a loose ponytail. Minimal makeup. The kind of presence that made the place feel warmer without changing the lights at all.

Fonzie's tail thumped faster. Alen's heart did something similar.

"Stacy!" Li Aiwen called. "Your usual?"

"Please," Stacy said, smiling as she came to the counter. She glanced around, caught sight of Alen and Fonzie, and her face brightened a little more.

"Hey, Alen," she said, walking over. "Hey, Fonzie."

Fonzie woofed once, as if claiming the credit for bringing her over.

Stacy's gaze dropped to the table. "Whoa. Did you make that?"

Alen forced himself not to cover it with his arms. "Yeah. It's, uh, for Sherri." He tried to sound casual and absolutely did not. "Every petal has a fortune. You know, romantic stuff. Or whatever passes for it in mass-produced cookie wisdom."

She picked up the flower gently, like it might bruise. "It's beautiful," she said. It wasn't the automatic compliment people gave to crafts; it sounded like the word cost her something. "She's going to love it."

Something flickered across her face then-small, quick, almost invisible. A flash of *I wish someone would make something like this for me* that she probably didn't even know leaked out.

Alen pretended not to see it. His chest felt weirdly tight.

"I'm just stuck on the last petal," he admitted. "I want something that actually means something. Not 'YOUR LUCKY NUMBERS ARE 3, 7, AND 9.'"

"My order came with a cookie," Stacy said. "Maybe the universe wants in on this."

She cracked the cookie open with practiced fingers, fished out the strip of paper, and read it aloud:

"*Peace within your heart will guide you to what's true.*"

The restaurant seemed to hush around the words. Even the clatter from the kitchen softened.

Alen swallowed. The sentence landed in him like a small, bright stone sinking to the bottom of a very deep pool.

"That's... perfect," he said, surprised at how much he meant it.

She handed him the fortune, and their fingers brushed. It was barely a touch, but his hand tingled afterward like he'd grabbed a live wire.

Li Aiwen slid a takeout bag onto the counter. "Beef lo mein, extra spicy," she called.

"Thank you," Stacy said, though her eyes stayed on Alen a second longer than on the food. "Good luck with your gift."

"Thanks," he said, standing and tucking the final fortune into the last petal. "See you around."

The bell chimed again as he stepped out into the evening, Fonzie trotting proudly at his eels.

Stacy watched the door swing closed, the paper flower still in her mind's eye.

Li Aiwen bumped her lightly with an elbow. "You should talk to him more," she said. "He has a good heart."

Stacy's cheeks warmed. "Yeah," she said softly. "I know."

CHAPTER TWO

Neon and Shadows

The bass inside Club Neon didn't just shake the floor; it rearranged ribcages.

Pink, green, and electric blue lights carved through cigarette haze, painting everyone in stuttering color. Bodies pressed together on the dance floor, slick with sweat and perfume and bad decisions.

In a dark corner booth, Sherri was kissing Troy like she was trying to leave teeth marks on his soul.

Troy-tall, smirking, smelling like cologne and trouble-pulled her closer by the waist. She laughed into his mouth, fingers curled in his shirt like claws.

Across from them, Mallory nursed a soda with the solemnity of a priest watching a sin.

"Sherri!" Mallory sputtered finally. "What about Alen?"

Sherri broke the kiss with a satisfied noise. Her lipstick was smudged; she wiped it with her thumb, using Troy's cheek as a mirror.

"Oh, please," she said. "Alen's sweet. He's like... a golden retriever in human form. But he kisses like he's apologizing."

Mallory winced. "You're going to burn in hell."

"Then I hope they serve margaritas," Sherri shot back. She turned to Troy. "You'll visit me on weekends, right?"

Troy grinned. "Count on it."

She slid out of the booth, tugging her skirt down and tossing her hair like she could shake off whatever guilt she had left.

"I'm going to get Alen," she said. "If he doesn't come with me tonight, I'm done."

Mallory opened her mouth to answer, but the DJ slammed the needle down on their song.

Matthew Wilder's "Break My Stride" exploded from the speakers.

Sherri and Mallory shrieked.

"This is OUR song!" Sherri yelled.

They threw their hands up and sang at the top of their lungs:

"Ain't nothin' gonna break my stride! Nobody's gonna slow me down-oh no-"

Then, clutching their chests dramatically, the secret alternate lyrics:

"I've GOT to keep my BOOBIES!"

Their laughter bounced off the mirrored walls, wild and irreverent.

Sherri wiped a tear from her eye. "Okay, now I'm going," she said, breathless. "Guard the booth with your life."

She strutted toward the exit, neon streaks sliding over her hair.

Outside, the night hit her hard-cold air, wet pavement, the muffled thump of bass through brick.

She wrapped her arms around herself. "Alen better answer," she muttered, turning down the alley that ran along the side of the club, phone already in hand.

She had no idea the choices she'd just made inside-Troy's hands, that kiss, those thrown-away words-had already shaken something loose in a boy who was, at that moment, desperately trying not to fall apart.

She had no idea that somewhere else in town, a quiet girl with warm eyes and a fortune-cookie smile had already taken root in that boy's heart.

CHAPTER THREE

The Doomsday Call

Fonzie knew something was wrong before the phone even rang.

He paced the bedroom in frantic loops while Alen dug through a chaotic mountain of gears and wires. The corgi's ears pinned back, his gaze flicking nervously between his human and the half-built machine on the workbench.

The thing blinked at them-a blinking red LED lodged in a tangle of springs and bent metal. It looked like someone had tried to build a robot, panicked halfway through, and just kept adding parts until it stopped asking questions.

The phone rang, shrill and insistent.

Alen nearly dropped a handful of screws. "Fonzie, shh," he said automatically, snagging the receiver. "Hello?"

"Alen." Sherri's voice was sharp and loud, cutting through the line like static. "I've been calling forever. Where *are* you?"

"I'm-uh-home," he said, heart rate spiking. "Are you okay?"

"No, I'm freezing and pissed off," she snapped. "Mallory ditched me. I walked all the way from the club. I'm stuck in that creepy alley by Neon. You need to come get me. Now."

His mind flipped through worst-case scenarios like a slide projector. "You want me to pick you up?"

"No, genius, I want you to serenade me from space. Yes, come get me. And Alen?"

"Yeah?"

"Don't do anything stupid before you get here."

The line clicked dead.

He stood there for a second, the dial tone buzzing in his ear, the words echoing in his chest.

Don't do anything stupid.

He hung up slowly and looked at the mess on his workbench.

The past year crowded into the room with him-the funeral, the half-finished inventions, his mother's shouted disappointments, Sherri's comments that stung like slaps.

He kisses like he's apologizing.

You need to grow up.

Try harder.

His hands moved before his brain caught up. He reached for scrap metal, bolts, bits of old toys, anything within reach. He needed to build. Not something useful. Just... something that could hold all the noise in his head.

Springs. A knob. Broken switch. Wire. The blinking LED. He twisted and stacked and screwed everything together in a frantic blur.

Ten minutes later, he was holding a monstrosity.

It rattled in his grip, heavy and pointless and ugly. Wires stuck out at random angles. The red LED blinked steadily, like a tiny, accusing heart.

"It's perfect," he whispered hoarsely. "It's terrible, but perfect."

His chest clenched. His breath shortened.

"I'm going to lose her," he said to the empty room.

Fonzie whined low in his throat.

The LED blinked again.

Alen shoved the contraption into his jacket pocket like a talisman-or a bomb-and grabbed his keys.

He paused at the door, fingers on the knob, panic humming along his ribs.

Then he stepped out into the night.

The door shut behind him with a soft click that sounded, in his head, exactly like the start of something breaking.

—-

CHAPTER FOUR

Impact

Fonzie sat tensely in the backseat as Alen's car cut through the dark streets. The corgi's gaze flicked constantly between the road and his human, a canine dashboard warning light that wouldn't turn off.

Alen spotted Sherri before his brakes fully caught up with the idea of stopping.

She stood in the wash of his headlights, arms folded tight, one foot tapping, her breath curling white in the cold air. Her expression said *I dare you to be one second later*.

He slammed the car to a halt. She yanked the passenger door open and dropped inside without looking at him.

"Finally," she snapped, slamming the door hard enough to rattle the mirror. "Do you have any idea how long I've been waiting?"

"I came as fast as I could," he said, fingers white-knuckled on the steering wheel.

She flipped down the visor and checked her reflection with a huff. "You always disappear into that little world of yours."

He pulled away from the curb. The streetlights slid over the dashboard in slow, pale bars.

Fonzie gave a low, warning rumble from the back.

"What's wrong with you?" Sherri said, finally looking at him. "You're twitching like you drank three pots of coffee."

"I'm fine," he lied. "Just... worried. You said you were stranded."

"I was," she said. "Mallory ditched. The club was a zoo. I am not walking home alone in heels. My feet hate me enough as it is."

He nodded, more apology than agreement.

Silence fell, thick and edged.

"You could've answered sooner," Sherri said after a beat. "I swear, sometimes you vanish into that garage and it's like you forget I exist."

"I was working on something," he said quietly.

"A toy?" she said, the word bending with contempt.

"It's just an idea. I don't even know what it is yet," he said.

She rolled her eyes. "Alen. You're twenty. You can't keep hiding behind gizmos and scrap metal forever. Get a real job. Do something real."

Every word landed like a hammer.

"I'm trying," he said.

"Well, try harder."

He blinked fast, the road starting to blur around the edges. He pressed his fingers tighter into the steering wheel, as if he could crush the panic into the plastic.

"Are you high?" Sherri demanded suddenly. "You're breathing weird."

"No, I just-" He swallowed. "I'm overwhelmed."

"By *what*?" she said. "Picking up your girlfriend? Poor baby."

The wave crested.

Grief. Quinn's headstone. His mother's endless shouting. The job rejections. The guilt. The fear Sherri was right, that he would always be almost something.

His chest seized. His vision tunneled.

"Alen," she snapped, "if this is some emotional meltdown-"

"Please," he managed. "Not tonight."

Then he choked on a sob.

It ripped out of him, raw and startled, like it had been hiding under his ribs and suddenly decided it was done waiting.

"You're crying?" Sherri stared at him, incredulous. "Are you serious? Alen, stop. You're embarrassing me."

Fonzie let out a small, distressed bark.

Alen's breaths came in short, broken gasps. The streetlights smeared across the windshield.

"Pull over," Sherri said sharply.

He didn't hear her.

"Alen! PULL. OVER."

The command snapped through the panic. He swerved to the curb and stomped the brake. The car jerked to a stop.

For a moment, the only sound was his ragged breathing and the faint thump of Club Neon in the distance.

Sherri slapped her hand against the dashboard. "Unbelievable. I can't deal with this."

"I'm sorry," he whispered. He meant it in about a thousand directions.

She looked at him like the apology itself was offensive.

"You know what?" she said. "Maybe I should've stayed at the club."

Something in him cracked in a way that felt permanent.

She flung the door open and climbed out. "I'm walking," she announced. "I can't sit in here while you... do this."

"Sherri-"

The door slammed shut.

Her heels clicked furiously down the sidewalk until the night swallowed her whole.

Alen stayed where he was, hands limp on the wheel, tears spilling over, hot and humiliating.

He pressed a palm flat against his chest like he could keep his heart from falling out.

If he didn't break on purpose soon, he was going to shatter by accident.

And he had no idea what would be left if that happened.

—-

CHAPTER FIVE

The Breaking Point

By the time he pulled into the driveway, Alen's whole body felt like a bad connection-everything shaky, sparks of fear jumping out randomly.

The house loomed ahead, a dark rectangle with two tired windows and a porch light that flickered whenever the wind disagreed with it. Inside, it always smelled faintly of coffee, bleach, and arguments that never ended.

He stepped through the front door and made it exactly three strides into the living room before the world tilted sideways.

The panic hit full-force.

His knees buckled. He caught himself with his hands, palms scraping the carpet.

"No. No, no, no," he gasped. "Please, not again-"

His chest tightened into a fist. The room shrank around him. The air felt thick, like breathing through cotton.

Footsteps crashed toward him.

"WHAT IS WRONG WITH YOU NOW?" His mother's voice split the air.

Dolores Bronte stood in the doorway, hair pinned back in a messy knot, dish towel in one hand, anger simmering in her eyes.

He tried to speak. "I-I can't-" The words snagged on his breath. "I can't breathe-"

"Of course you can't breathe," she snapped. "You work yourself into these... theatrics. Just like your father."

The panic twisted sharper at that.

Fonzie darted in, sliding on the rug, and planted himself between them with a sharp, protective bark, his little body low and bristling.

Dolores threw her hands up. "I swear to God, Alen, sometimes I wish I'd never had you."

The sentence landed harder than any slap.

His lungs gave up.

He folded in on himself, shaking, tears blurring the ceiling into watery streaks. Shame crashed over him, nasty and hot.

"I can't do this," Dolores muttered, turning toward the phone. "I'm calling someone to deal with you."

He heard the receiver lift. Heard her start dialing.

A sharp knock rattled the front door.

Dolores slammed the phone down and stomped to the entryway. "Who now?"

She yanked it open.

Sherri stood on the porch, arms crossed, makeup intact, hair perfect. She looked mildly annoyed. Not cold. Not scared. Not grateful.

"Hey," she said, stepping past Dolores without waiting to be invited. "My ride ditched me again. Can I come in?"

Dolores scoffed. "Apparently, everyone needs rescuing tonight," she muttered, but moved aside.

Sherri walked in and stopped dead.

Alen was on the floor, chest heaving, face wet, Fonzie pressed against his side like a furry life preserver.

"What happened to you?" she asked, more puzzled than concerned.

He tried to pull himself together, to sit up, to look like something other than an emotional car crash in front of the girl he still stupidly loved.

"Sherri, I-I made something for you," he said. The words wobbled, but they were all he had. "It's in the garage. I just need to show you-"

He staggered to his feet, clinging to the wall as he made his way toward the door that led to his makeshift workshop. Fonzie stayed glued to his heel.

Sherri followed, her expression somewhere between curiosity and *this better be worth my time*.

The garage was chaos. Wires, gears, tools, blueprints. Half-built devices and fully broken dreams.

In the center of it all, perched on a table, stood his latest masterpiece of madness: a towering, precarious Rube Goldberg contraption made from scrap metal, pulleys, mousetraps, and that same blinking red LED at its heart.

His Doomsday Machine.

The moment he stepped near it, something clicked.

A marble rolled down a track with cheerful inevitability. It hit a spoon, which flipped into a spring, which launched a ping-pong ball, which smacked into a mousetrap, which snapped.

The mousetrap jerked a string.

The string yanked a lever.

The lever swung a metal arm directly into Alen's ankle.

He yelped and toppled backward into a pile of junk, sending a cascade of gears and springs clattering over him.

Sherri burst out laughing.

"Oh my God," she wheezed. "What even *is* this? Are you auditioning for America's Funniest Home Videos?"

Her laughter sliced something tender inside him.

His breath hitched. His hands started shaking again.

"Sherri, I'm not-I'm not okay," he said. The room was spinning. "I-"

She rolled her eyes. "And this is why I can't take you anywhere."

Dolores appeared in the doorway, face tight. "He's having another episode," she announced. "I called the hospital. They're sending someone."

"M-Mom, no," Alen pleaded. "Please. I just need-"

"Enough," she snapped. "You are going. I am done dealing with this."

The panic surged again, big enough to swallow him whole.

He hit the floor a second time.

Somewhere in the blur:

Paramedics. Boots thudding. Voices issuing calm instructions. Cold plastic on his skin. Straps tightening.

Sherri stood against the hallway wall, arms crossed, watching it unfold like a boring movie she couldn't change the channel on.

She didn't say goodbye.

She didn't say anything.

They wheeled him past her and out into the waiting night.

As the gurney rolled toward the ambulance, the world narrowed to a tunnel.

In that tunnel, one memory glowed:

A small slip of paper. Warm hands. A voice soft as the inside of a secret.

Peace within your heart will guide you to what's true.

Stacy's face drifted up through the panic, and for a second, he held onto it like a rope.

Then the doors closed.

The siren wailed.

And the city swallowed him whole.

CHAPTER SIX

White Rooms and Flickering Lights

The ambulance rattled down the street like a shopping cart on a freeway.

Bright lights. Sharp smells. Velcro, plastic, and the steady beep of a monitor that seemed personally offended by his pulse.

Fonzie sat on the gurney near Alen's hips, harness clipped hastily to a rail. He let out a sharp bark every time the paramedic adjusted a wire, as if to say, *Hands off my human, lab coat.*

"This is a terrible time to die," Alen thought, watching the ceiling shake overhead. "I haven't even returned my library books."

An oxygen mask settled over his face. The paramedic-a guy with a mustache that deserved its own zip code-leaned over him.

"Just relax, okay?" the man said.

Relax.

He'd been body-slammed by his own invention, humiliated in front of Sherri, screamed at by his mother, and hauled out of his house like a broken appliance.

Relax didn't even have a forwarding address in his brain right now.

The ambulance doors flew open. Hospital light poured in-too white, too bright, like God had flipped the "on" switch too close to his face.

"My retinas," Alen muttered. "They're gone. Vaporized. Tell them I loved them."

The nurse pushing his gurney didn't even slow down. "Happens all the time," she said.

It absolutely did not.

They rolled him into an exam bay. Machines sprouted from the walls like metallic ivy. A blood pressure cuff latched onto his arm and squeezed with the kind of enthusiasm reserved for overly friendly relatives.

A doctor appeared. Mid-forties, tired eyes, good posture.

"You're having an acute panic episode," he said.

"No, that's... that's normal for me," Alen said. "This is standard. Factory settings. Very healthy. Very on brand."

"You passed out twice," the doctor replied.

"I'm an enthusiastic napper," Alen offered.

The nurse snorted. The doctor did not.

A syringe flashed in the fluorescent light.

"Nope," Alen said. "No, thank you. I'm allergic to needles."

The nurse paused. "You are?"

"Emotionally," he clarified. "And possibly spiritually."

Warmth flowed into his arm anyway. His limbs went pleasantly heavy. The ceiling stopped spinning like a bad game show wheel.

When he opened his eyes again, the world had changed.

Quieter. Softer. No more frantic beeping, no more rush of gurneys.

He was in a small room with padded walls and a soft blue blanket. The clock ticked politely. The overhead light hummed.

A sign on the wall read:

PSYCHIATRIC OBSERVATION UNIT.

"Oh, come on," he groaned. "I was unconscious for, what, five minutes? You can't just lock a guy in the Quiet Room because he trips over a mousetrap."

The door opened.

A nurse stepped in, clipboard under her arm. Early thirties, curly hair pulled back in a bun that had clearly lost several battles today. Her badge read **MARLENA**.

"Good afternoon, Alen," she said. "Welcome to the quiet room."

"This room isn't quiet," he said. "It's aggressively calm. I feel like a ghost is about to offer me herbal tea and unsolicited advice."

Marlena sat on the chair near the bed, flipping a page on her clipboard. "We're just going to keep an eye on you overnight. Make sure you're stable. Check in on your thoughts. Your breathing. Whether you decide the wallpaper looks tasty."

"I'm not going to eat the wallpaper," he said.

"Good," she replied. "You wouldn't be the first, though."

He blinked. "That... doesn't make me feel better."

She smiled, just a little. "This isn't punishment," she said. "It's just... a pause button. Your brain hit fast-forward for too long. We're helping it rewind."

He stared at the ceiling.

"I'm not crazy," he said.

"I didn't say you were," she replied.

"It feels like everyone else did."

She studied him for a moment. "You had a bad night," she said. "Bad nights lie. That's their specialty."

He let out a breath that sounded suspiciously like a laugh.

She patted the side rail lightly. "Get some sleep," she said, standing. "The doctor will talk to you in the morning. In the meantime, my official medical advice is: no inventing new ways to set yourself on fire."

"Harsh," he said. "But fair."

She dimmed the lights and left.

He lay there, listening to the soft buzz of the fluorescent and Fonzie's quiet snuffles from a dog bed in the corner where the staff had reluctantly agreed he could stay.

The panic had drained away, but something else sat in its place. Hollow. Heavy.

He closed his eyes.

A slip of paper floated up behind his eyelids. Stacy's voice. Her smile.

Peace within your heart will guide you to what's true.

He turned the sentence over in his mind, worn and worried like a coin in a pocket.

For the first time since the night began, the world didn't feel like it was pressing down on his lungs.

For the first time in a long time, he felt the smallest, most fragile thing:

Not okay.

But maybe... not doomed.

—-

CHAPTER SEVEN

Release and Residue

By morning, the hospital hallways hummed with fluorescent light and the sterile smell of disinfectant - a smell that had started to cling to Alen's hair, his clothes, even his thoughts.

Fonzie had not slept. Not really.

The corgi spent the night patrolling the tiny room as if guarding a fragile treasure. Every so often he'd stand with his nose pressed to the side of the bed, checking that Alen was still there, still breathing, still reachable.

When the doctor finally cleared him for discharge, Fonzie bounced anxiously from foot to foot, like a furry pressure cooker about to explode with relief.

And then Dolores arrived.

The energy in the room changed instantly - the air pulling tight like a rubber band stretched too far.

She swept in with theatrical exhaustion, gold bracelets clacking, lipstick flawless despite claiming she'd barely slept. She immediately spotted the doctor down the hall and angled toward him, voice lifting into something fluttery and far too familiar.

"Doctor," she gushed, brushing a hand over her hair, "thank you for taking such good care of my son. If there's ever anything - *anything* - I can do..."

Fonzie froze mid-pacing. His ears flattened. His tail went stiff. He watched her the way a dog watches a vacuum cleaner right before it tries to suck up his favorite toy.

The doctor excused himself with an expression best described as *politely fleeing*, leaving Dolores deflated and annoyed.

"Let's go," she said briskly, grabbing Alen by the elbow.

He winced. "Mom, can you... maybe not-"

"Come ON, Alen." She tugged harder, as if she could drag him back to sanity through sheer force.

Fonzie growled. Low. Vibrating. A warning.

Dolores shot the dog a glare. "Oh, hush, you little sausage."

But when she reached for Alen again, Fonzie stepped between them, body stiff, blocking her path.

Tiny. Determined. Unbowed.

"Fonzie - move," she snapped.

He didn't.

Alen touched his head gently. "It's okay," he murmured. "He's just... trying to help."

Dolores rolled her eyes but released her grip.

The three of them walked out of the hospital together - Alen exhausted, Fonzie hyper-alert, Dolores muttering about "dramatic tendencies" under her breath.

They reached the parking lot. Dolores shook her keys impatiently.

The car ride started in silence. Three minutes of it, long enough for Alen to believe maybe - *maybe* - she would soften.

But Dolores Bronte was not built for silence.

"So," she said sharply, "was collapsing really necessary? You embarrassed me in front of a VERY handsome doctor."

Alen closed his eyes. "Mom..."

"And did you SEE his arms? My God. That man could bench-press a refrigerator. I might finally have found someone worthy of me - but no, you just had to melt down everywhere."

"Mom."

She waved the comment away like a fruit fly. "Well, whatever. Water under the bridge. You're alive, I'm annoyed, life goes on."

Fonzie whined in protest.

They drove two more blocks before she suddenly swerved toward the curb and parked. Hard.

Alen opened his eyes, alarmed. "What are we-"

"I forgot," she said, rummaging through her purse. "I have that appointment. You'll slow me down. Get out."

He stared at her. "What?"

"Out!" She pointed at the sidewalk. "You're discharged! Walk it off!"

"Mom, I just got out of a psychiatric-"

"EXACTLY. You need fresh air. Goodbye!"

Before he could protest, she reached across him, opened the passenger door, and gave him a firm shove.

He stumbled onto the sidewalk.

The door slammed.

The tires squealed.

She was gone.

The street fell silent except for a distant bird and the far-off hum of traffic.

Alen stood there for a long moment, stunned, Fonzie pressed warm against his leg.

"...She really left me," he whispered.

A passing jogger lifted two fingers in a sympathetic salute. "Moms, man."

Alen let out a weak, incredulous laugh.

Then he squared his shoulders, wiped his eyes, and started walking.

He didn't know where he was going.

But he knew he wasn't going back.

—-

CHAPTER EIGHT

The Highway and the Red Convertible

The highway stretched ahead of him like a long, sun-baked dare. Heat shimmered above the asphalt, warping the air into a wavering mirage. Alen trudged along the shoulder, sweat plastering his shirt to his back, dust sticking to his shoes.

Fonzie trotted faithfully at his heels, occasionally stopping to sniff at a discarded soda can or bark at a fence post that looked suspiciously like a threat.

A cow in the adjacent field watched them with deep bovine judgment.

Alen wiped sweat from his forehead. "Don't look at me like that," he told the cow. "I'd like to see you have a panic attack and get abandoned on Route 9."

The cow mooed, unimpressed.

He kicked a pebble. It skittered across the melting blacktop, bouncing to a stop.

Then - the sound.

An engine. Growing louder. Closer. The kind of throaty, confident rumble that usually belonged to people whose lives were significantly more glamorous than his.

A cherry-red convertible burst through the heat haze.

Wind in its hair. Sunshine in its teeth. Glamour in its exhaust fumes.

It screeched to a stop beside him in a flourish of gravel and synth-pop.

"HEY, ALEN!" a voice yelled.

Mike leaned over the wheel, aviator sunglasses reflecting the entire world back at Alen. In the backseat, Tori waved a beach towel like she'd captured it in a daring raid.

And in the passenger seat - hair wild from the wind, sun turning her skin gold-

Stacy.

She leaned her elbows on the door. "We're going to the beach!" she called. "Waves, sand, total freedom. Want in?"

Alen blinked. "I have... urgent business with this pothole," he said, pointing solemnly at the cracked asphalt near his foot. "It's auditioning for its big break. I can't just abandon it."

Tori snorted. Mike slapped the steering wheel laughing.

Stacy smiled gently. "Drama king," she said, holding out her hand. "Come on. Let the pothole pursue its solo career."

There was something in her voice - a warmth, an invitation - that cracked him open in a small but significant way.

He took her hand, climbed into the backseat, Fonzie scrambling after him, and the convertible peeled away in a blur of sunlight, wind, and sudden possibility.

For the first time in days, Alen felt the world open wide enough for him to breathe.

—-

CHAPTER NINE

M1 Beach

The main stretch of M1 Beach was chaos - umbrellas, radios, sunscreen, surfers, families shouting over sandcastles and sandwich wrappers.

But Stacy tugged Alen toward a narrow path lined with bending sea oats. Driftwood stood like sculptures guarding the entrance. The further they walked, the quieter the world became.

"This is the good part," Stacy said, snorkel mask pushed onto her forehead, flippers clacking softly. "Before the crowds. Before the noise."

Alen adjusted his own gear nervously. "Just so you know, if a fish looks at me wrong, I'm going back to shore."

She laughed - a sound that lifted the whole afternoon.

"Trust me," she said. "This place is magic."

They rounded a curve of rock and the view hit them like a held breath released:

A hidden cove.

Water in shades of turquoise and emerald.

Sunlight filtering through it like falling coins.

A lagoon cradled by rocks and whispering sea grass.

"Oh," Alen breathed.

"Right?" Stacy grinned.

He stepped into the water beside her. It was cool, clean, forgiving.

She dove first - smooth, graceful, a streak of pale limbs and bright fins. He followed, awkward for the first few seconds until the water wrapped around him and the world above vanished.

Underwater, everything slowed. Softened.

Coral glowed like underwater fireworks. Fish darted past in neon flashes. Light danced across the sand below their feet.

Stacy tapped his shoulder and pointed to a crevice.

An octopus rested there - small, curious, its skin shifting from brown to shimmering blue as they approached.

One tentacle reached out slowly.

Alen's heart thumped in wide-eyed wonder.

He gave Stacy a clumsy underwater thumbs-up, bubbles spiraling from his grin.

For the first time in a long time, he wasn't afraid of anything.

Not the ocean.

Not panic.

Not being alive.

—-

CHAPTER TEN

After the Water

The living room smelled faintly of sunscreen and ocean salt. Beach towels draped over chairs like sunburned ghosts. Fonzie lay sprawled on the floor, belly-up, snoring blissfully-the official sign of a successful day.

Alen sat on the couch, damp hair curling, face more relaxed than Stacy had seen in months.

"You look lighter," Stacy said softly, sipping from a glass of iced tea. "Like the ocean washed some of the heavy off you."

He shrugged, embarrassed but not denying it.

"Probably the sunburn," he said. "Or maybe that you ambushed me with Karen Carpenter."

"You hummed along!" she accused.

"Purely reflex," he said. "She's irresistible."

She laughed-and then the laugh melted into something gentler.

"Today was different," she said. "You were different."

Alen stared at his hands.

"It's been a long time since I felt okay," he admitted. "Not since... not since Dad."

She nodded, leaning closer but not pushing. "Tell me about him."

He hesitated.

Then - he did.

And the room seemed to listen.

—-

CHAPTER ELEVEN

Quinn

The toy store smelled like plastic and cardboard and the kind of artificial strawberry that didn't exist in nature.

Little Alen - five years old, bowl-cut slightly crooked - stood in the middle of it all, vibrating with joy. Shelves towered over him: Transformers, Micronauts, G.I. Joe, Cabbage Patch Kids, every box a portal to somewhere better.

"Pick one, champ," Quinn said.

His dad was all flannel shirts and soft stubble and tired eyes that still somehow lit up whenever he looked at his son. He leaned one elbow on the cart, watching Alen with pure, amused interest.

"Just one?" Alen said, scandalized.

Quinn laughed. "Two, then. One to save the world. One to destroy it."

Alen took this extremely seriously.

He chose a Transformer - all chrome and promise - and a G.I. Joe with a scar on his face and a grenade launcher bigger than his torso.

Quinn paid, then ripped open the Transformer's box right there in the aisle. He transformed it in three smooth motions, making laser noises under his breath. Nearby shoppers smiled without meaning to.

"Ready for battle?" Quinn asked.

"Micronauts, roll out!" Alen yelled, mixing up franchises with the confidence of someone who didn't recognize intellectual property lines.

They played right there, in the middle of the store. Just a man and his kid and two pieces of plastic staging an epic war over a sale bin of Barbies.

"Just you and me, kid," Quinn said.

For a long time, it was.

They were a two-person universe: backyard baseball at dusk, burgers on a dented grill, forts made from couch cushions, late-night Atari marathons until the TV hummed with ghost images after they turned it off.

In the garage, under a bare bulb, Quinn taught him how to solder wires without burning his fingers. How radios worked. How electricity didn't care about feelings but still somehow felt like magic.

"Everything talks if you listen right," Quinn would say, tapping a circuit board. "You just gotta learn the language."

Then, one ordinary afternoon, the universe changed.

Quinn was flipping burgers, smoke curling up into a blue sky. Alen was on the steps, sorting tiny screws into mismatched jars.

There was a thud.

A spatula hitting the deck.

When Alen looked up, his father was crumpled on the porch, one arm twitching, the other limp.

"Dad?" Alen said.

No answer.

"Dad!"

The world blurred: his mother screaming, the phone call, sirens, the blur of hospital hallways and beeping machines and doctors speaking in a language much harder than circuits.

Quinn survived the stroke. Technically.

He came home with one side slack and heavy, words coming out thick and slow. The house, once filled with motion and noise, became a minefield of silence and unspoken fear.

Alen sat in the garage with a notepad, hands shaking as he sketched gears and joints and wires.

If the problem was broken signals, he would build something that shouted for the brain. A harness, maybe. Motors to move the arm. A device that would give his dad back what the stroke stole.

He cobbled together parts from toys, junk, anything with a motor. When he wheeled the contraption into the living room, heart pounding, Quinn was in his old armchair, staring woodenly at the TV.

"Dad," Alen said, setting the device on the coffee table. "This will help. It'll move for you until you can on your own."

Quinn's eyes warmed. Crooked smile. "You're something else, kid."

Dolores walked in, took one look, and snapped, "We are not turning this house into a science fair. Put that junk away."

"It's not junk," Alen said. "It can help him."

"We have doctors," she snapped. "We do not need your... toys."

She grabbed for the device. One of the wires snapped. The whole thing sagged in on itself, dead.

Something broke in Alen that never quite healed.

The last time he saw his father alive, Quinn was back in that hospital bed, light too harsh above him.

"Love you, mustard seed," Quinn murmured, voice thin but fond. "Don't stop building weird things. The world needs 'em."

Then his hand went slack in Alen's.

The funeral was gray - sky, suits, faces. Alen clutched the remnants of the failed device in his backpack, the weight of it like a confession.

He'd been too slow. Too small. Too late.

Somewhere inside him, a quiet vow hardened:

Next time, he'd be ready.

—-

CHAPTER TWELVE

Teardrop Falls

The waterfall at Delphi Mountain was the opposite of a hospital.

The air was cool and wet and alive, smelling like wet stone and pine needles. Water poured over the rock face in silver ribbons, breaking into mist that kissed their skin.

Stacy stood near the edge of the pool, sneakers damp, hair curling from the spray. She looked fully in her element - like big, loud places made her shrink but wild, quiet ones made her expand.

"Some people call this Teardrop Falls," she said. "But the older stories say it's the place where White Buffalo Woman cried for the people. Her tears became the water. Healing water, you know?"

Alen sat on a rock, knees drawn up, listening.

"She shows up when people forget who they are," Stacy went on. "Reminds them how to live with respect. With heart."

She crouched and sifted through the slick, smooth stones at the edge of the pool, fingers moving with easy familiarity.

"Hold out your hand," she said.

He did.

She placed a small stone in his palm. Smooth. Pale. Shaped like a slightly lopsided heart.

"Teardrop Falls tradition," she said. "You keep it when you need courage." She tapped it lightly. "Proof the water sees you."

Something in his chest tilted. The trees whispered above them. The waterfall roared. And in the middle of all that noise, there was a pocket of quiet just big enough for a realization:

He was in love with her.

Not the way he'd loved Sherri - frantic and apologetic, chasing approval like a dog chasing headlights. With Stacy, it was... different. Less like a cliff dive, more like finally realizing you'd been standing in a river all along.

"Stacy," he said, the name catching on a suddenly dry throat.

She looked up at him.

He leaned forward and kissed her.

Soft. Careful. Not a question. Not stolen.

A promise.

For a second, the world fell perfectly still.

No hospital monitors. No shouting. No humming neon. Just the sure press of her mouth against his, the damp air, the steady thunder of the falls.

When they pulled apart, her eyes were wide and bright, not startled so much as seeing something at a new angle.

"Wow," she whispered.

He laughed, dizzy with relief and terror. "Yeah."

Then - like a lightning bolt through wet branches - the idea hit him.

"Crystal bioamplifier," he blurted.

She blinked. "What?"

"The water. The stone. The way signals travel," he said, words tumbling over each other. "I've been thinking too small - I can amplify the bio-signals, not just carry them. I have to-"

He scrambled off the rock, nearly tripping over a root.

"I have to write this down," he said. "Before it leaves. Stacy, I-"

He stopped himself.

She watched him, half amused, half wounded, as he backed away.

"Alen-"

"I'll call you," he said. "I swear. I just-if I don't draw this out, it'll evaporate."

Then he was gone - crashing through the trees, heart hammering with equal parts invention and fear.

Stacy stood alone by the falls, the spray freckling her cheeks.

She pressed her fingers to her lips, then curled her hand protectively around the place his mouth had been.

"Of course," she murmured. "You'd sprint away right after that."

But she was smiling.

She'd gotten used to loving people who ran toward their ghosts.

—-

CHAPTER THIRTEEN

Blueprints and Faultlines

Sunlight slanted through the blinds in thin gold stripes, pooling over the chaos on Alen's living room table - half-drunk coffee, bits of wire, the good pencils he only used when things mattered.

The heart-shaped stone from the falls sat on the corner of his sketchpad, holding the page in place like a tiny, defiant paperweight.

He drew furiously.

Signal tracings. Muscle fiber. Sensor placement. Waveforms. Notes in the margins about comfort and weight and cost. A crystal bioamplifier that wouldn't just move a limb but coax the body into relearning its own language.

"This time," he muttered under his breath, "I'll get there in time."

The front door banged open.

Gordon drifted in, his hair in that perpetual just-rolled-out-of-someone's-bed look, a smirk half-formed like his default expression. He tossed a stack of mail onto the coffee table.

"Mail call," he announced. "From the land of debt and despair."

Alen didn't look up. "If it's a bill, it's not for me. I've transcended the concept of money."

Gordon picked up one of the sketches, whistling low. "This for fun, or are you finally inventing something that can pay rent?"

"Stroke recovery," Alen said. "For real this time. Sensors, feedback, game interface... it could work, Gordon. Not just for Dad. For other people like him."

Gordon's mouth tightened almost invisibly at the mention of Quinn.

"You and your salvage projects," he said lightly. "You know you can't fix everything with duct tape and microchips, right?"

"Watch me," Alen said.

Gordon dropped an envelope with a corporate logo in front of him: **KRONOS NOVELTIES, INC.**

"This one, though... that might fix other things," he said. "You got a letter."

Alen froze.

He recognized the name, the stylized K. He'd met one of their reps at the mall - Katelyn with the sharp lipstick and sharper eyes - who'd said things like "innovative mind" and "exciting opportunities" and "think about it."

His heart thudded as he tore it open.

"Dear Mr. Bronte... impressed by your designs... offer of employment... Kronos Innovation Division..."

His breath caught.

"Holy shit," he whispered. "They want me."

Gordon's smile didn't reach his eyes. "Congrats," he said. "You're officially a corporate drone."

Alen barely heard him. His mind had already sprinted three steps ahead.

Kronos meant money. Labs. Real tools. A shot.

It also meant leaving.

"Stacy kissed me," he blurted suddenly, brain skidding lanes. "At the falls. I think I'm... I think I'm in love with her."

Gordon's jaw flexed. "Wow," he said. "Moving fast, huh?"

"I'm gonna ask her to come with me," Alen said, half to himself. "To the city. Or... ask her to wait until I get settled and then come. Or... something. I don't know. I just... I don't want to do this without her."

"Maybe," Gordon said slowly, "you get settled first. Make some cash. Prove you can keep the lights on. If you ask her now, it might sound... desperate."

The word stung.

Alen stared at the letter, mind wobbling.

"Yeah," he said finally. "Yeah, maybe you're right."

Gordon clapped him on the shoulder. "Of course I'm right."

Later that day, Alen took his sketches and the heart-shaped stone to Stacy's porch. He placed them gently into her hands, eyes bright.

"You inspired this," he said. "For my dad. And for anyone like him. This-this is the start."

She looked down at the drawings, at the little stone, then back up at him with a softness that made him immediately want to run and stay at the same time.

"Promise me something," she said.

"Anything."

"Keep moving forward," she said. She reached out and tapped the center of his chest. "Even when it's heavy. Especially then."

"I promise," he said.

Words crowded his throat. *Come with me. Let's build a life. I love you.*

None of them made it out.

"I should go," he blurted instead. "Call to make. Stuff to... you know. Sort."

"Alen-"

But he was already backing down the steps, heart pounding, fear louder than love.

She watched him go, thumb brushing over the heart stone, blueprints fluttering slightly in the breeze.

When he turned the corner out of sight, she tied the sketches and stone together with a ribbon and tucked them into a small package.

For later, she thought.

For when he was ready to hear what he already knew.

—-

CHAPTER FOURTEEN

City Lights

The city smelled like hot pretzels, car exhaust, cheap perfume, and opportunity.

Alen stepped off the bus with one duffel bag, one portfolio case, and one corgi in a travel crate who was loudly protesting the concept of confinement.

"Big leap, buddy," Alen murmured.

Fonzie huffed.

Kronos Novelties occupied a gleaming corner of the mall, all chrome racks and blinking gizmos and cardboard cutouts of extremely enthusiastic people holding extremely questionable products.

"Don't be a stranger, Alen," Katelyn said, her lipstick a precise slash of red. She'd met him on his tour, heels clicking like punctuation marks. "You and I? We're going to make each other rich." She tapped his chest lightly with a manicured finger. "If you don't let that conscience of yours get in the way."

Before he could reply, someone caught his elbow.

He turned, nearly losing his footing on a slick spot of tile.

"Easy there, dreamer," a woman said, steadying him.

Short dark hair. Sharp suit. sharper gaze.

She handed him the business card that had just slipped from his fingers.

"Alen Bronte," she read. "Nice handwriting."

"Mira Herz," she added, nodding toward her own card. "Attorney."

"Is that a threat or a promise?" he asked, half-joking.

"Free advice," she said. "Companies like Kronos? They'll wrap you in neon and call it family - right up until they smell a way to make more money off you than with you." She jerked her chin toward the food court. "Come on. I'm legally required to buy anyone I lecture a cup of coffee."

Chrome Moon Diner was a retro fever dream - red vinyl booths, shiny chrome trim, a jukebox in the corner playing Elvis just a little too loudly. Twin waitresses in matching beehives - Terri and Lori - darted between tables.

Terri gave him a once-over. "New in town," she declared. "Has that 'I sold my soul to a mall job' look."

"He'll toughen up," Lori said, dropping menus. "Or implode. Either way, we'll see him a lot."

Over fries and coffee, Alen told Mira more than he meant to: about Quinn, about the failed device, about the crystal bioamplifier idea, about Stacy at the falls.

"I just want to build something that matters," he finished lamely. "Something that actually helps people instead of... I don't know. Selling plastic misery machines."

"That's what all the good ones say," Mira said. "Right before someone higher up decides their dream would look better with a corporate logo stamped on it."

She slid her card across the table.

"Do yourself a favor," she said. "Call me before you sign anything you don't understand."

He nodded. "I will."

He actually meant it.

For now, though, the city was big, the future was bright, and the part of him that still felt like a kid in a toy store was louder than the part that remembered hospital lights.

—-

CHAPTER FIFTEEN

Gordon's Lie

Back home, the town looked smaller without Alen in it.

Stacy stood on the porch of his apartment building, package in hand - the blueprints and heart stone neatly tucked inside, a handwritten note of her own folded between them.

She knocked.

The door opened a crack.

Gordon filled it, leaning one shoulder casually against the frame.

"Hey, Stacy," he said. "Alen's not here."

"I know," she said. "I heard he left for the city. I just wanted to drop this off. For when he gets back. Or... whenever."

Gordon's smile hardened at the edges. "Yeah, about that. He's not coming back."

Her fingers tightened around the package. "Did he say that?"

"He left yesterday," Gordon said. "No goodbye. No note. Just grabbed his stuff and bolted." He shrugged. "Some people aren't big on... closure."

The air went thin.

"No call?" she asked quietly. "No message for me?"

"Nothing," Gordon said. Then, as if remembering something: "But, hey, you look great. If you ever want to-"

Fonzie padded into the hallway behind him and barked, sharp and urgent, cutting him off.

Stacy flinched - not from the sound, but from the sudden clarity.

"Tell him I stopped by," she said, voice flat, turning away.

"Sure," Gordon said.

He wouldn't.

Stacy walked home with the package still in her arms. She placed it carefully on her dresser, tracing the ribbon with her fingertip.

She didn't open it.

She couldn't.

Not yet.

CHAPTER SIXTEEN

Little Buffalo

Stacy stood at the front of her third-grade classroom with a crayon drawing held in one hand and the other keeping a fragile kind of order.

"Okay," she said with a smile that softened all the kids around her, "one more time from the top."

They sang.

Badly.

Joyfully.

Loud enough to rattle the hamster cage in the corner.

"Row, row, row your boat..." they chorused, voices wobbling in a chaotic round, some arriving early, others late, some shouting like the song was a battle cry.

Jenny - perpetually enthusiastic, perpetually off-key - belted, "LIFE IS BUT A DREAM!" with enough force to startle the gerbil in the next classroom.

Stacy laughed, wiping tears from her eyes because joy did that to her sometimes.

Then a tiny gasp cracked the room's bubble of happiness.

Emily - small, solemn, the kind of child whose silences said more than other kids' paragraphs - knelt beside Old Mr. Hickory's cage. Her wide brown eyes stared down at the still little body inside.

"Ms. Stacy?" she whispered. "He's not... moving."

Silence spread like spilled paint.

Stacy crossed the room, knelt next to her, and gently closed the cage door. "Okay," she murmured, "everyone back to the rug."

They sat cross-legged, faces tilted up like small moons.

"Is he dead?" Tommy asked, blunt the way children are when adults aren't listening.

Stacy nodded once.

A wave of emotions pulsed through the group - confusion, sadness, dread, curiosity.

"Death is confusing," Stacy said. "It's not wrong to feel lots of things at once."

"Why do things have to die?" Emily asked, voice trembling.

Stacy considered the question. She could've given them a soft, vague answer - something about life and cycles and comfort. But kids deserved truth wrapped in gentleness, not avoidance.

"Well," she said, "some people believe our souls don't just disappear. They keep learning. Growing. Like metal in a forge - each life is a hammer tap that shapes us. That idea's called *gilgul*. A soul's journey."

A few kids gasped softly - the kind of gasp that meant their imaginations were unfolding.

"And there's another story," Stacy continued, "from the Lakota people. About White Buffalo Woman. She teaches that love and kindness don't stop when someone dies. They keep going. They become part of the world in ways we can't always see."

Emily sniffled. "But what about Mr. Hickory?"

Stacy smiled gently. "Maybe he'll come back as something bigger. Stronger. A buffalo with a huge heart."

Jenny raised her hand. "Will he still like sunflower seeds?"

"I don't think that part ever goes away," Stacy said.

Later, as the bell rang and backpacks thumped and sneakers squeaked down the hall, Raymond lingered near her desk.

Shy. Quiet. Sweater sleeves too long.

"Ms. Stacy?" he whispered.

"Yes, Raymond?"

He held out a crumpled drawing. A hamster wearing a crooked crown. Beside it: a buffalo with a huge, ridiculous heart drawn across its chest.

"This is you," he said. "'Cause you said buffalo have big hearts. So... you're like Little Buffalo."

Before she could speak, he blushed tomato red and sprinted out of the room.

Stacy held the drawing against her chest.

Little Buffalo.

The name settled into her bones like a tiny blessing.

—-

CHAPTER SEVENTEEN

Parents and Promises

A few days later, with sunset turning the classroom windows honey-gold, Stacy was hunched over spelling tests when Principal Edwards stuck his head in.

"Stacy? Raymond's parents are here. Want to talk to you."

Her stomach dipped. Parent meetings could go either way.

In the hallway, a couple stood waiting - Liam and Amy Miller. Warm eyes. Soft voices. Worry lines etched into kindness.

Raymond stood between them, nervous but hopeful.

"Mrs. Stacy," Amy said, "we wanted to thank you."

"Thank me?" Stacy echoed. She glanced at Raymond, who stared at his shoes.

"You helped him," Liam said. "He came home talking about souls and buffalo hearts and... courage." His voice cracked a little. "He stood up for himself at recess today. First time ever."

Raymond peeked up at her.

Stacy knelt to his height. "You did that?" she whispered.

He nodded. "It was hard."

"But you were brave," she said. "That's what matters."

Amy touched Stacy's arm. "You're the kind of teacher we prayed he'd get. We just wanted to tell you that."

The praise hit something tender inside Stacy - a place that still felt shaped by all the ways her own childhood had lacked this softness.

She swallowed. "Thank you. I love these kids. I mean that."

When the Millers left, Stacy returned to her empty classroom, the drawing of Little Buffalo propped on her desk.

She imagined - just for a reckless second - a future where she had this kind of family. Where kindness wasn't something she had to teach so much as breathe.

She imagined Alen there too - laughing, tinkering, dog underfoot. A home filled with the kind of love that didn't get drowned out by yelling.

CHAPTER EIGHTEEN

The Letter

Days later, she stood at the post office counter, the small package resting on the scale.

"City address, huh?" the clerk said, slapping on a label. "Big changes."

"Something like that," Stacy murmured.

She sent the package to Alen's new apartment, then headed to the community center, where she taught eight-year-olds how to talk about loss without falling apart.

Life, for the moment, moved forward in uneven steps.

When the box arrived at Alen's place, it sat untouched for two days on the table by the door. He passed it every morning on his way to work, every night on his way to bed—always noticing, never opening.

Alen sat at the small dining table in his new apartment, the city humming faintly through the balcony door. In front of him lay a half-filled page—his handwriting uneven from everything he was trying to say at once.

Stacy,

I should've told you sooner. About the job. About the move. About how things are finally steady enough that... if you wanted... you could come here. With me.

I'm not running from you. I'm trying to build something worthy of you.

He paused, pressing his fingers to his eyes. This wasn't how he'd imagined the start of their next chapter. The goodbye he never gave her still gnawed at him.

A knock jolted him.

Before he could stand, the door opened and Katelyn slipped inside, leaning heavily on the frame. Her hair was mussed, her smile loose around the edges.

"Guess who brought a little celebration?" she sang, lifting a paper bag with a bottle inside. "Thought you might want company in your fancy new place."

"Katelyn..." He straightened, wary. "Are you drunk?"

"Tipsy," she corrected with a giggle. She swayed closer, too close. "But not too tipsy to see that you look lonely."

"I'm fine," he said, stepping back. "Really."

Her eyes dropped to the letter on the table. "Writing love notes? Didn't know you had it in you." She traced a finger across the page like she had a right to. "You know... you don't have to be alone tonight."

He angled himself away. "Katelyn, stop."

She blinked, surprised—and offended.

He stood, folding the finished page carefully and placing it beside the envelope. "I need to mail this. Then I should probably call it a night."

Katelyn recovered quickly, smoothing her hair and her expression. "Well, if you want, I can take it to the post office. I'm heading that way tomorrow."

He shook his head. "No. I can do it."

Her smile twitched. "Sure. Whatever you say... babydoll."

He didn't react to the nickname. He'd long since stopped noticing her little flirts.

And in the kitchen, while he reached for tape, she acted.

She moved silently, slipping the true letter into her purse and replacing it with a blank sheet from his printer stack. Same size. Same weight. Same crisp fold.

By the time he returned, she had already sealed the envelope.

"I taped it up for you," she said lightly. "Thought I'd help."

He took it without suspicion. "Thanks."

His phone rang.

He answered without looking at the screen. "Hello?"

Silence.

Then: her voice, fragile and unsure. "Alen?"

"Stacy?" Relief cracked through him. "Hey—I've been wanting to talk to you."

A chirpy voice rose in the background on his end, bright and teasing.

"Babydoll did you want get you something to drink from the kitchen"

Katelyn knew what she was doing.

Alen's stomach dropped. "Wait—Stace, that's not—"

Her breath hitched. "Wow," she said softly, a quiet blade wrapped in cotton. "Okay. Got it."

"Stacy, please. It's not what you think, she just—"

"Why are you playing with my feelings?" The words were barely a whisper.

"I'm not. I swear, just listen—"

But the line had already gone dead.

He stared at the phone, disbelief turning slowly into something hotter, sharper.

He turned toward Katelyn, who was lounging in the doorway, twirling a strand of her hair, smug beneath the veneer of concern.

"What?" she asked, all faux innocence.

His voice came out low, controlled only by effort. "Get out."

She blinked. "Excuse me?"

"You heard me. You crossed a line tonight. Leave. Now."

Her expression curdled—shock slipping into anger, then into something mean—but he didn't look away.

After a long, brittle silence, she grabbed her bag and stormed out, the door slamming behind her.

Alen sank into the nearest chair, the phone still in his hand, dread pooling in his stomach.

Something was wrong. Something he didn't see coming.

CHAPTER NINETEEN

The Doom Box

Kronos Novelties had two faces.

The public one was glossy - bright kiosks, shiny packaging, commercials with kids laughing too hard at things that weren't funny.

The internal one was hungrier.

Alen discovered that version in the Innovation Lab - a big room lined with workstations, prototypes, and enough fluorescent light to tan a corpse.

Romulus and Remus ruled that space.

The twins - not actually Roman, not actually mythic, but determined to act like they were - wore matching pinstripe suits and matching predator smiles. They'd been with Kronos just long enough to believe the company's worst habits were virtues.

"Our baby," Romulus said grandly one afternoon, unveiling a monstrous contraption on a wheeled cart.

The Doom Box.

TV screen. Boombox. Cassette deck. Built-in phone cradle. Panels for tabloids. A glittery compartment labeled "Secrets." Lights that blinked for no discernible reason.

"It's a one-stop culture injection system," Remus said, slapping the top like a used car salesman. "Pipelines for engagement, emotional manipulation, and recurring billing."

"Looks like a Decepticon with a gambling problem," Alen muttered.

Katelyn laughed too loudly. "Ignore him," she said, linking her arm through Romulus's. "The kids will eat this up. Especially the girls. We'll market it as a wish machine or something. 'Open the box, open your destiny.'"

"Or 'ruin your credit,'" Alen said under his breath.

No one seemed to hear him.

Except Mira.

She appeared in the lab doorway that afternoon like an alarm bell in heels, holding a folder and wearing the expression of someone who'd already read all the terrible fine print.

"Remember what I said?" she murmured as he walked her back to the hall after her meeting with HR. "Neon family, real teeth."

He nodded numbly.

He'd been so focused on repairing things - his father's legacy, his own guilt, the misunderstanding with Stacy - that he'd walked straight into the arms of a company designed to use dreamers like batteries.

He just didn't know how bad it was yet.

—-

CHAPTER TWENTY

Kronos at Its Worst

The Kronos corporate party was held in a rented ballroom lit by neon and bad decisions.

Music pounded. Drinks flowed. Executives pretended to be human for an evening.

Alen slipped to the fringes, clutching a soda and wondering when, exactly, his life had become a collage of mall lights and moral nausea.

He passed an open office door and heard it: Katelyn's voice, sharp and low.

"Pandora's Box for girls," she was saying. "You draw them in with wishes and gossip. Secret compartments, 'dream boards,' whatever. Get them obsessed with image. Beauty. Desire. They'll beg their parents for more upgrades."

A man's voice answered - Rosendo, one of the senior execs. Smooth. Disgustingly calm.

"And for the boys," he said, "we lean on violence. Fighting games. Celebrity scandals. Build their identities around the stuff we sell them. We've already got interest from private detention contractors. Behavioral conditioning disguised as entertainment? They love that stuff."

Alen froze in the hall.

His stomach turned.

This wasn't just sleazy. It was structural.

"Stroke-recovery prototype?" another voice asked - one of the twins.

"Already reverse-engineered," Rosendo replied. "Nicely done, boys. The legal department drafted the IP claim. Our name's on it now."

Something inside Alen snapped.

He stormed into the doorway.

"You stole my design," he said, voice shaking but loud enough to cut through the music.

Rosendo looked mildly amused. "We developed a device based on inspiration from multiple sources."

"I showed you those blueprints," Alen said. "I built that for my dad. For people like him. You slapped your logo on it and gutted the ethics."

"You signed the contract," Rosendo replied, sliding a document toward him. "Right here. 'All ideas conceived during employment'-"

"-belong to Kronos," Mira finished from the hallway.

She stepped in behind Alen, eyes cold.

"Cute," she said. "Did you also mention the coerced overtime and intentionally confusing language? Or did that get left out of the party chatter?"

"This is a private event," Rosendo said. "You're not invited."

"Neither is intellectual theft," Mira shot back.

Security arrived like summoned storm clouds.

They escorted Alen and Mira out - gently enough not to cause a scene, firmly enough to make the point.

The neon sign outside the building flickered as they stood on the sidewalk, dazed.

He had lost the device. He had lost Stacy. He'd lost his sense of what the future was supposed to look like.

All he had left was grief, a corgi, and a handful of people who believed him when he said this shouldn't be how the world worked.

And, he realized, that might be enough to start a war.

—-

CHAPTER TWENTY-ONE

Stacy's Fate

The call came at night.

He was packing - what little he had - when the phone rang, sharp and shrill.

"This is Alen," he said, trying to sound like a person who had his life together.

"Alen... it's Tori," came the reply. Her voice was thin, thready. "You need to come home."

He sank onto the arm of the couch. "What happened?"

"It's Stacy," Tori said. A pause. "Cancer. Fast. Aggressive. The doctors... they're not optimistic. She keeps asking for you."

The world narrowed.

"I'll be there," he said. "I'm coming now."

The trip back blurred-bus, then borrowed car, then sprinting down too-familiar hospital corridors that all smelled like his father's last days.

He found Stacy's room by instinct more than signage.

She was smaller.

The illness had thinned her, pale skin stretched over sharp bones. Her hair - once a sunlit halo - lay in wisps against the pillow. The room hummed with machines and swollen quiet.

Tori stood at the foot of the bed, eyes red.

"Hey, Little Buffalo," Stacy whispered, voice barely there, as Alen stepped inside.

He choked on a laugh-sob hybrid. "That's my line," he said, dragging a chair up to the bed and taking her hand.

Her fingers were cool but still undeniably hers.

"I sent you my whole heart," he said. "In a letter. Did you get it?"

Tori's face tightened. "She got... a blank one," she said quietly. "An empty page."

"No," he said, shaking his head. "I wrote it. Every word. I told you I loved you. I told you about the device, the falls, about wanting you to come with me. I... I wrote everything."

Stacy smiled faintly. "It's okay," she murmured. "I think... I knew anyway."

He pressed his forehead to her hand. "I'm so sorry. For leaving. For not calling. For... all of it."

She squeezed his fingers weakly. "We're all just... doing our best," she said. "Sometimes our best trips on the stairs."

A small cough shook her.

He wiped her lips gently with a tissue.

"Do you remember," she whispered, "when the kids kept asking me why death... why we have to go?" Her eyes drifted, seeing a classroom he'd never been in. "I told them souls are like metal... hammered and shaped... life after life. Gilgul."

"You told me that too," he said.

"Feels like my soul's been in the forge for a while," she said, trying to joke. It came out thin.

An alarm beeped once, then reset.

"Sing to me?" she asked suddenly. "Like you did at the falls."

He blinked back tears. "What, like... Springsteen?"

She smiled. "The first song," she whispered. "The one we joked about. The one the kids... always wanted."

His throat tightened.

"Row, row, row your boat," he began, voice unsteady. "Gently down the stream..."

She mouthed the words with him.

"Merrily, merrily, merrily, merrily..."

"Life is but a dream," she whispered.

The monitor stuttered.

Then went flat.

The room didn't explode or collapse. It just... emptied.

Something vast and invisible lifted out of the space, and he was left holding her hand and the echo of a song.

Tori's sob broke the spell.

Alen bowed over Stacy's still fingers and cried like something in him had finally shattered all the way through.

—-

CHAPTER TWENTY-TWO

Ashes and Whiskey

The bar was dim, smelling like old beer and older secrets. A Springsteen song murmured from the jukebox, tired but stubborn.

Alen sat hunched over a glass of whiskey that he kept forgetting to drink.

Fonzie was at his feet, chin on his shoes, silent in a way that hurt.

"What's the point?" Alen said quietly, to the glass, the bar top, the universe. "I tried, and I still lost her. I tried with Dad. With the device. With Kronos. Everything I touch just... breaks."

"Sounds like you need new material," a voice said to his right.

The man who'd taken the barstool beside him looked the same as he did that day he showed up with the mail at the psych ward.

"Harold Mercury Godwin," he said, offering a hand. "Everyone calls me Mercury. You look like you're auditioning for a tragedy."

Alen shook his hand weakly. "you look like I know you from somewhere."

Mercury nodded toward the untouched whiskey. "She wouldn't want you to quit," he said.

Alen swallowed hard. "You don't even know her."

"I've known a lot of hers," Mercury said. "Men like you, too. The ones who get knocked on their ass by life and start thinking lying down is a personality trait." He sipped his drink. "You loved her?"

"Yes," Alen said. No hesitation.

"Good," Mercury replied. "Means she did her work. People like that... they're like jumper cables. They shock you back into yourself. Hurts like hell. Wakes you up."

"I don't feel awake," Alen said. "I feel... hollow."

Mercury shrugged. "Hollow's just room for something new."

He slid a wrinkled napkin over. On it was scribbled the name and address of a law firm.

"Mira Herz, Esquire," Mercury said. "She came into the postoffice once, chewing out an insurance adjuster. Meanest angel I've ever seen. You still got that thing they stole from you?"

"The device?" Alen said. "They have the prototypes. The patents. Everything."

"But do you have *your* work?" Mercury asked. "Original sketches? Dates? Anything that proves you were you before Kronos pretended they made you up?"

Alen thought of the shelf in his apartment.

The unopened package.

Stacy's handwriting.

He sucked in a breath.

"Maybe," he said.

"Then don't drown here," Mercury said, standing. "Fight in a room where the rules mean something."

He slapped a few bills down for his drink and walked out, leaving the napkin like a small, dangerous blessing.

Alen stared at it.

Then at the door.

Then at the reflection of his own tired face in the bar mirror.

"Well," he told that reflection. "Guess we're not done yet."

Fonzie thumped his tail once, as if in agreement.

—-

CHAPTER TWENTY-THREE

The Law Firm

Two days after Stacy's funeral, grief and fury braided so tightly inside Alen that he could barely breathe.

But there was clarity too. A sharp, narrowing focus.

Kronos had stolen his work.

Stacy had died believing he'd given up.

His father had slipped away before he could help him.

Nothing he did now could change the endings.

But he could fight for the living meaning behind them.

So he walked through the glass doors of **Rhea, Emmett & Associates**, Mira's firm. The place smelled like paper, toner, and legal battles fought by people who actually knew what justice was supposed to look like.

Mira met him in a conference room with a stack of case files under one arm and her hair pulled back in a no-nonsense twist.

Omar, her junior associate - quick-witted, sharp-minded - sat beside her, tie crooked, pen tapping restlessly.

Alen laid his sketchbooks on the table.

"These are mine," he said. "Originals. Dated. I wasn't sure they mattered before. But Kronos took everything and twisted it. They're selling a corrupted version of my design."

Omar flipped through pages, eyebrows rising. "This is... incredibly detailed."

"He did this before Kronos ever touched him," Mira said, nodding.

"They'll fight dirty," Omar warned. "They'll claim ownership. They'll manufacture timelines."

Alen looked down at his hands. "I want to do this," he said. "For my dad. For Stacy. For every person who needs that device. I'm tired of letting things get stolen from me."

Mira sat back, a slow, fierce smile forming.

"Then let's make them regret ever underestimating you."

CHAPTER TWENTY-FOUR

Dolores

Before he could fight Kronos, there was one more door he had to open.

One more ghost to face.

The house looked smaller than he remembered. The air inside - lavender, dust, old grief - hit him like a memory wrapped in barbed wire.

Dolores answered the door, dish towel in hand, makeup perfect out of habit more than necessity.

"Alen," she breathed, startled but cautious. "You didn't call."

"No," he said. "I didn't."

Dr. Faex Buco - her new boyfriend, kind eyes behind wire-rimmed glasses - stood behind her, steady but silent.

The living room was exactly the same: the indentation where Quinn used to sit, the crooked portrait on the wall, the half-finished radio gathering dust.

The ghosts were loud.

"Mom," Alen began, before he could lose his nerve. "You yelled at him. You yelled at me. You shut him down. You shut me down. He needed help, and I was trying, and you-"

Dolores flinched.

Tears welled - unexpected, uninvited.

"I was miserable," she whispered. "I didn't know how to cope. I took it out on him. On you. I've replayed that day a thousand times. I was wrong. I was... cruel. And I'm sorry."

Silence expanded - heavy, fragile.

Alen's throat tightened. "Why didn't you say that before?"

"Because I didn't know how," she said. "And I was afraid you wouldn't listen."

Dr. Buco stepped forward gently. "You're fighting for something good now," he said to Alen. "Don't drown in old pain. Let it be part of your strength."

Alen nodded slowly.

"I'm not doing this just for me," he said. "I'm doing it for the people I lost - and for who I'm still becoming."

Dolores touched his cheek, hand trembling. "Then go," she said. "Win."

CHAPTER TWENTY-FIVE

Courtroom Tides

The courtroom was packed - journalists, curious townsfolk, Kronos execs in expensive suits, students from Stacy's school who'd somehow convinced bus drivers to bring them.

Mira stood at the plaintiff's table in a navy suit sharp enough to cut glass. Omar had six binders open and color-coded like a battlefield map.

Alen sat between them, palms sweaty but steady.

Across the aisle sat the Kronos team.

Polished. Predatory.

Rosendo in the front row like a smug kingpin.

Katelyn beside him, posture perfect, eyes calculating.

The hearing began.

Kronos's lawyer stood first, voice smooth as oil.

"Your Honor, this is simple. My clients created the recovery device. Mr. Bronte is an ex-employee who seeks undeserved credit."

They produced blueprints - doctored, altered - designed to look older than Alen's.

They spoke in words meant to intimidate: proprietary, derivative, prior art.

Then Mira stood.

"Your Honor," she said, "they stole from him."

She summoned witnesses, cross-examined executives, dismantled timelines.

Omar presented Alen's sketches, dated pages showing progress over years - fragile proof of a dream that predated Kronos's greed.

The judge frowned.

"It is compelling," she said, "but inconclusive."

Mira stiffened. "We're missing something," she whispered to Alen. "Something original. Something time-verified."

A ripple moved through the crowd.

In the back row, someone stood up.

Harold Mercury Godwin.

Wearing a T-shirt with a white buffalo on it.

He waved and Alen noticed the white buffalo T-shirt. It triggered something deep inside Alen.

Alen froze.

The unopened package.

Stacy's handwriting across the label.

"It's dated," Mercury mouthed the words. "Unopened. Sent before Kronos filed anything."

Alen exhaled shakily. "Stacy mailed me some of the early blueprints. Before everything went sideways. Before Kronos stole it." He swallowed. "I never opened the package. I couldn't."

Mira's eyes sharpened. "Then that package might be the key. Time-stamped. Untampered with."

A gasp rippled through the room.

The judge ordered a brief recess.

The package was retrieved and opened with ritual precision - in plain view, carefully documented.

Inside:

The original blueprints.

Alen's handwriting.

Dated.

Stamped by the postal service.

And a sealed note from Stacy.

The courtroom held its breath as the judge opened it.

Her voice softened as she read:

"Alen -

I'm sending these because you created something beautiful and I don't trust the world to protect it the way you would. Keep going. Don't let them take this from you.

- Stacy."

The judge looked up.

"Mr. Bronte," she said slowly, "this is decisive. The court finds that Kronos Novelties did misappropriate your intellectual property. The rights to the recovery device revert fully to you."

The gavel cracked like thunder.

Cheers erupted.

Reporters surged.

Security scrambled.

Katelyn stood, face stunned.

Rosendo cursed under his breath.

Romulus and Remus looked like malfunctioning robots.

Alen just sat there, hand over his mouth, tears pricking hot behind his eyes.

Mira leaned down, voice soft.

"She saved your work," she whispered. "Even after everything. Even when she didn't get to see this."

Alen closed his eyes and saw the waterfall again - Stacy's hand pressing a heart-shaped stone into his palm.

He whispered, "Thank you."

—-

CHAPTER TWENTY-SIX

Re-Animation

1994.

The Re-Animation office smelled like hope and solder.

Old CRT monitors glowed in shades of turquoise and amber. Controller cables coiled like lazy snakes across desks. Posters of underwater landscapes - reefs, kelp forests, tide pools - lined the walls.

Alen stood beside a woman in her sixties. Her right arm had been weak since her stroke. She flexed her fingers slowly, hesitantly.

"Ready?" Alen said gently.

She nodded.

He strapped the lightweight sensor device to her forearm. On the screen, the virtual world flickered into view:

A shimmering underwater reef.

Color blooming everywhere.

Sunlight drifting in beams.

Fish darting past in neon bursts.

Reef of Dreams.

She moved her fingers.

Her avatar swam.

Her breath hitched. "It feels like I'm flying," she murmured, eyes bright with wonder.

In the corner, Omar scribbled notes like a man tracking a miracle in real time.

"Motor responses up twenty percent," he said. "This is going to change everything."

Mira leaned in the doorway, watching with a smile that wasn't her usual sharp-edged smirk.

"You did it," she said quietly.

"No," Alen said, adjusting the woman's strap gently. "We did it."

In the corner, Fonzie - older, muzzle frosting with white - snored contentedly on a blanket made from old T-shirts.

When the session ended, the woman hugged Alen with her good arm. "You gave me back a piece of myself," she whispered.

After she left, Omar turned to Alen. "Once we finish the home version, think of the people we'll reach. Folks who can't afford hospitals. Or live too far to travel."

Alen nodded, eyes distant but warm.

"Life is but a dream," he said softly.

"What?" Mira asked.

"Nothing," he said. "Just... a reminder."

—-

EPILOGUE

Echoes of the White Buffalo

The waterfall at Delphi Mountain looked almost exactly the same as the day Stacy had kissed him there.

Almost.

The trees were a little taller.

The rocks a little rounder.

The grief inside him - lighter, reshaped.

Alen stood at the overlook, the heart-shaped stone warm in his pocket.

"Thank you," he whispered into the mist. "For the stone. For the reef. For the courage. For the future."

A hand slipped into his.

Mira.

Hair wild from the wind, boots scuffed from the hike, eyes soft but steady.

"Talking to ghosts again?" she teased gently.

"Always," he said.

Below them, Fonzie bounded along the water's edge as energetically as his little legs still allowed. Children splashed in the shallows - a boy skipping stones, a girl shrieking with delighted laughter.

Their mother waved at Alen as he came down the path.

"I'm Amy," she said. "This is Liam. And these two troublemakers are Raymond and Stacy."

The name landed in his chest like a bell.

The girl - Stacy - wrapped her arms around Fonzie's neck with fearless affection.

"Stacy," he echoed softly. "That's... a beautiful name."

Amy smiled. "Someone very special to us had it first."

As they walked toward the path, little Stacy tugged on her mother's sleeve.

"Mom," she whispered loudly, glancing back at Alen. "That was Mr. Mustard Seed."

Amy blinked. "What?"

"Nothing," the girl said with a secret grin.

Up the path, Mira watched Alen's face soften with a kind of peace she hadn't seen before.

The waterfall roared.

The mist shimmered.

The world breathed.

Alen lifted the heart-shaped stone from his pocket and let the water lap at its edges.

Every moment - every fall, every heartbreak, every invention, every love - had hammered his soul into a shape truer than the one he began with.

A shape Stacy would have been proud of.

A shape Quinn had believed in before anyone else did.

Life was still messy. Still cruel in places. Still unpredictable.

But it was also beautiful.

And fragile.

And stubbornly full of grace.

"Ready?" Mira asked, lacing her fingers with his.

He looked down at the stone, then at the water, then at the trail leading toward whatever came next.

"Yeah," he said. "I'm ready."

They walked away hand in hand, Fonzie trotting ahead, the sound of the falls echoing behind them like a promise-

the White Buffalo Woman watching,

the water carrying every name,

and somewhere, in the quiet space between myth and memory,

Stacy's voice humming:

Life is but a dream.

THE END

Below is a detailed analysis of the esoteric meanings behind the names of characters, companies, and locations in the story "STACY" by Arnold Jackson. Drawn from etymology, mythology, biblical references, spiritual/esoteric traditions (e.g., Kabbalah, Lakota spirituality, neuroscience, and embryology), and the clues provided (e.g., M1 Beach as the Primary Motor Cortex, Alen as "tiny rock," and Mr. Mustard Seed linking to faith, the pineal gland's calcite microcrystal, and embryonic development). The story appears to be an allegorical tale blending personal grief, invention, and spiritual awakening. Esoterically, it explores themes of soul reincarnation (Gilgul), consciousness (pineal gland/third eye), brain function (motor cortex, neuroplasticity), faith as a "seed" for growth, and the journey from material illusion to spiritual enlightenment. The narrative mirrors embryonic development: the pineal gland's calcite crystal forms around 7 weeks, coinciding with the heart's first beat, symbolizing the soul's "incarnation" and awakening.

Key esoteric framework:

- **Pineal Gland/Third Eye**: Central motif. The calcite microcrystal (piezoelectric, responsive to electromagnetic fields) is linked to the "mustard seed" (tiny but powerful faith/enlightenment). It forms in embryos at ~49 days (7 weeks), then the heart beats—symbolizing the soul's entry into the body.

- **Reincarnation/Soul Journey**: References to Gilgul (Jewish mysticism: soul transmigration, refining like metal) and White Buffalo Woman (Lakota: brings peace, transformation; her "tears" as the waterfall symbolize compassion and non-suffering).

- **Brain/Consciousness**: Stroke recovery device represents neuroplasticity (rewiring the brain/soul). M1 Beach = Primary Motor Cortex (controls voluntary movement; "first drive" into physical action/incarnation).

- **Faith and Creation**: Mr. Mustard Seed (Matthew 17:20/Luke 17:6: faith moves mountains) ties to the pineal crystal's formation, embryonic heart beat, and invention as "creating life" (e.g., Alen's devices).

- **Overall Allegory**: Alen's journey = soul's evolution from loss/illusion (material world/Kronos) to healing/enlightenment (Re-Animation/resurrection). Stacy = guiding spirit/resurrection force.

Meanings Behind Names

Characters

| Name | Literal/Etymological Meaning | Esoteric Interpretation |

|———|——————————————————|———————————————|

| Alen | Variant of Alan; Gaelic/Irish: "little rock" or "handsome, cheerful." | The "tiny rock" clue points to the calcite microcrystal in the pineal gland (third eye/seat of soul). Alen represents the embryonic soul awakening—small but foundational. His inventions (stroke device, games) symbolize piezoelectric activation (crystal responding to pressure/faith). Journey from grief to creation mirrors soul refinement (Gilgul: metal hammered into sword). |

| Quinn Bronte (Father) | Quinn: Irish, "wise" or "intelligent." Bronte: Greek, "thunder." | "Wise thunder"—enlightened force, like a divine spark (thunder as God's voice in Bible). Represents paternal wisdom/soul legacy; his stroke = blocked enlightenment (pineal/heart disconnection). Calls Alen "Mr. Mustard Seed," linking to faith/pineal crystal. Death = soul transmigration. |

| Dolores (Mother) | Spanish: "sorrows" (from "Our Lady of Sorrows,"). | Embodiment of earthly suffering/illusion (Maya). Her nagging = material distractions blocking spiritual growth. Relationship with Dr. Faex Buco = false healing (sorrow tied to "dregs"). Later redemption = soul's journey toward compassion. |

| Sherri | Variant of Sherry; French "chérie": "darling" or "dear." | Superficial affection/illusion of love. Her betrayal = ego-driven desires (Club Neon as artificial light/false enlightenment). Contrast to Stacy's true resurrection love. |

| Stacy | Greek: "fruitful" or "resurrection" (from Anastasia). | Central esoteric figure: resurrection of the soul. Teaches reincarnation (Gilgul, White Buffalo Woman). Her cancer/death = sacrificial transformation; sends heart-shaped rock (pineal crystal/faith seed) and blueprints (soul blueprint). Reincarnates as little Stacy in epilogue (soul cycle). Song "Row Your Boat" = life as dream/illusion (Maya), gently navigating reincarnation stream. |

| Li Aiwen | Chinese: Li = "plum" (beauty/endurance); Aiwen = "love" + "literature/culture." | "Loving wisdom/beauty"—elder guide (like oracle). Restaurant = nourishment for soul; fortune cookie = serendipity/divine message ("peace within your heart"). Sparks Alen-Stacy connection (pineal awakening). |

| Troy | Greek: From Troy (city in Iliad, symbol of war/deception). | Betrayal/ego conquest (cheats with Sherri). Represents base instincts blocking spiritual path. |

| Mallory | French: "Unfortunate" or "ill-omened." | Harbinger of misfortune/illusion. Enables Sherri's betrayal = complicity in material traps. |

| Fonzie (Dog) | From "Happy Days" character (cool, loyal); Italian "Alfonso": "noble and ready." | Loyal guardian spirit/animal totem. Barks warnings (intuition/third eye). Corgi = earthy, short-legged (grounded in physical world but alert to spiritual threats). |

| Harold Mercury Godwin | Harold: "Army ruler." Mercury: Roman god of messengers/tricksters. Godwin: "Friend of God." | Divine messenger (Hermes/Mercury). Delivers "fate" (origami flower/fortunes) = angelic intervention. Sports analogies = life's "game" (soul lessons). "Man upstairs" = God; encourages perseverance (soul refinement). |

| Tori | Japanese: "Bird" (freedom/spirit); or Victoria: "Victory." | Bird as soul messenger (victory over death). Stacy's roommate = supportive guide in reincarnation lessons. |

| Raymond | Germanic: "Wise protector" or "protecting hands." | Child soul learning protection/kindness. Calls Stacy "Little Buffalo" = recognizes her as White Buffalo Woman avatar (peace/compassion). Reappears in epilogue = soul continuity. |

| Old Mr. Hickory (Hamster) | Hickory: Strong, resilient wood; "Old Hickory" = Andrew Jackson (toughness). | Class pet = innocent soul vessel. Death teaches reincarnation (Gilgul: soul as metal refined). Transforms to "buffalo" (strength via love). |

| Dr. Faex Buco | Latin: Faex = "dregs/feces" (waste). Buco/Bucco = "mouth/cheek." | "Fecal mouth"—false healer/charlatan (wasteful words). Seduces Dolores = illusion of comfort in sorrow. Contrast to true healing (Alen's device). |

| Mike | Hebrew (Michael): "Who is like God?" | Archangel-like protector. Drives to beach = initiates spiritual journey (M1/motor cortex awakening). |

| Gordon | Scottish: "Great hill" or "spacious fort." | Earthly obstacle (hill to climb). Jealous roommate = ego sabotage (lies about Alen). |

| Katelyn Birsha | Katelyn: "Pure." Birsha: Biblical (Genesis 14), king of Gomorrah = "son of wickedness." | False purity masking (evil) (Sodom/Gomorrah destruction). Saboteur = demonic force (steals letter, twists inventions). "Pure Evil"|

| Mira Herz | Mira: Latin "wonderful/admirable/Peaceful" Herz: German "heart." | "Wonderful heart"—compassionate guide/love interest. Lawyer =

justice (scales/balance). Helps awaken Alen's heart (post-Stacy). "Peaceful Heart"|

| Terri and Lori | Terri: "Harvester." Lori: "Laurel" (victory/honor). | Twin forces of harvest/victory (reaping soul lessons). Diner = sanctuary/nourishment for spirit. |

| Rosendo | Spanish: "Famous path." | False path/illusion (Kronos leader). "Famous" = ego-driven fame. |

| Romulus and Remus | Roman mythology: Twins raised by wolf, founded Rome (fratricide). | Destructive duality (ego vs. spirit). Doom Box = technology as prison (wolf devouring innocence). The two systems of controling the mind in the world. Based on Compensatory control theory (CCT) Religion (Remus) and Political (Romulus)|

| Omer | Hebrew: "Sheaf" (first fruits/measure); Arabic "long-lived." | Measure of soul harvest 49 days (first fruits = pineal awakening). Game designer = creator of healing "realms." |

| Maria | Hebrew: "beloved" (Mary, mother of Jesus). | Divine feminine (angelic dancer). Reads Alen's "rhythm" = soul vibration/harmony. |

| Liam and Amy (Epilogue Parents) | Liam: "Resolute protector." Amy: "Beloved." | Protective love nurturing reincarnated souls (little Stacy/Raymond). |

| Little Stacy and Raymond (Epilogue Children) | As above. | Reincarnated souls (cycle complete). Little Stacy recognizes Alen as "Mr. Mustard Seed" = pineal faith seed. |

Companies

Name	Literal Meaning	Esoteric Interpretation
————	————————-	————————————
Kronos Novelties	Kronos: Greek Titan (time, devours children). Novelties: Trivial inventions.	Time as devourer (eats innovation/souls). Represents material illusion/trapping youth (Pandora's Box scheme = opening to evil/reincarnation traps). Contrast to Re-Animation (resurrection).
Rabbit Hole	From Alice in Wonderland: Descent into wonder/madness.	Esoteric initiation (down the hole to hidden knowledge/third eye). Novelty shop = superficial wonders masking deeper truths. Wasting of time.

| Chrome Moon Diner | Chrome: Shiny metal. Moon: Lunar/feminine, cycles/illusion. | Polished illusion (chrome as false light). Moon = reincarnation cycles; diner = soul nourishment/sanctuary. Twins = duality (harvest/victory). |

| Rhea, Emmett, and Associates | Rhea: Greek Titaness (mother of gods, wife of Kronos). Emmett: "Truth/universal." | Maternal protection/truth against devouring time (Kronos). Law firm = justice/balance in soul journey. Rhea, wife of Kronus, saved their son Zeus (also known as Jupiter in Roman mythology) from being swallowed by Kronus by deceiving him with a stone wrapped in swaddling clothes or package. .|

| Re-Animation | Re- (again) + Animation (bringing to life/soul infusion). | Resurrection of soul (reincarnation/healing). Games = simulated realms for soul training (neuroplasticity as spiritual rewiring). |

Locations

Name	Literal Meaning	Esoteric Interpretation
———	—————————-	—————————————
Oakwood Cemetery	Oak: Sacred tree (strength, Druids). Wood: Material form.	Gateway to afterlife/reincarnation. Cherry blossoms = renewal (soul cycle). Alen's visits = communing with father's spirit.
Chinese Restaurant (Wong's)	Wong: Chinese "king" or "yellow" (enlightenment).	Nourishment for awakening (fortune cookies = divine oracles). Meeting Stacy = soul connection.
Club Neon	Neon: Artificial gas light.	False enlightenment (bright but empty). Sherri's world = ego distractions.
Alen's Workshop/Basement	Basement: Subconscious depths.	Invention space = alchemical lab (creating life/soul devices). Doomsday Contraption = ego's self-destruction timer.
Mental Hospital	"Loony bin."	Mind's prison/illusion (padded walls = buffered reality). Green eggs and ham = absurd dream state (life as illusion).
Community Classroom	Community: Shared learning.	"Classroom of life" = reincarnation school (soul lessons via children/innocence). Hamster death = teaching transmigration.
M1 Beach (First Drive Outer Layer)	As clue: Primary (First) Motor (Drive) Cortex (Outer Layer).	Brain's motor area (voluntary action/incarnation into physical). Snorkeling = diving into subconscious (reef = neural networks;

octopus = intelligence/multitasking brain). Hidden cove = third eye awakening.

| Teardrop Falls (Delphi Mountain) | Teardrop: Tears/emotion. Delphi: Greek oracle. | White Buffalo Woman's tears = compassionate non-suffering. Waterfall = purification/soul cleansing. Heart-shaped stone = pineal crystal/love activation. Epilogue return = cycle closure. DMT, Christos oil, Deuteronomy 8:3, Matthew 4:4|

| The Mall | Commercial hub. | Material illusion/labyrinth (sensory overload = ego traps). |

| City Apartment | Urban isolation. | Transitional space (from small town/ soul origin to worldly trials). |

| Delphi Mountain Waterfall | As above. | Oracle of truth (prophecy/ enlightenment). Epilogue = full circle reincarnation. |

Table for Index and Lessons on Reading the Esoteric Side for fun.

Here are some suggestion for structured guide to encourage layered reading. Try to map chapters to esoteric elements, meanings, and lessons (how to interpret for spiritual insight). Use it to "decode" the narrative: Read surface plot first, then revisit with esoteric lens (e.g., characters as soul aspects, events as awakening stages).

Chapter	Key Esoteric Elements	Meanings/Symbols	Lessons for Esoteric Reading
————	——————————	————————	————————-
Prologue: Whispers from the Grave	Cemetery, father's headstone, cherry blossoms.	Renewal (blossoms), soul communication (whispers).	View grief as soul continuity; graves = portals to past lives. Lesson: Loss initiates awakening (pineal activation via emotion).
Chapter 1: Fortunes Folded in Petals	Fortune cookie, origami flower, "peace within your heart."	Serendipity/oracle, heart as guide (pineal-heart link).	Interpret meetings as fated (soul contracts). Lesson: Small acts (folding paper) = shaping reality/faith seed.
Chapter 2: Shadows in the Neon Glow	Club Neon, betrayal, "Break My Stride."	Artificial light = false paths; stride = motor cortex/action.	See ego relationships as illusions. Lesson: Discern true love (heart) from material distractions.

| Chapter 3: The Doomsday Contraption | Stroke device, Rube Goldberg machine, overload. | Neuroplasticity = soul rewiring; contraption = karma chain. | Accidents = divine interventions. Lesson: Overthinking (mind) leads to chaos; trust intuition (pineal). |

| Chapter 4: Padded Walls and Green Eggs | Mental hospital, green eggs (absurdity), Harold's fortunes. | Dream state/illusion (Maya); green = heart chakra. | Insanity = unawakened mind. Lesson: Use humor/absurdity to transcend (soul as "prototype in beta"). |

| Chapter 5: Lessons in the Classroom of Life | Hamster death, Gilgul, White Buffalo Woman, "Top of the World." | Reincarnation (metal refinement), compassion/tears. | Children = pure souls teaching adults. Lesson: Life's pains = hammer strikes forging strength; choose kindness. |

| Chapter 6: Mother's Prescription | Hospital release, mother's car argument, beach invite. | Maternal sorrow = earthly anchor; beach = motor awakening. | Family conflicts = past-life karma. Lesson: Forgive to free soul (tough love as catalyst). |

| Chapter 7: Currents of the Heart | M1 Beach snorkeling, reef/octopus, flashback to father. | Dive into subconscious (neural reefs); octopus = brain adaptability. | Memories = soul blueprints. Lesson: Love activates creation (heart-pineal link). |

| Chapter 8: Teardrop Falls and Heart-Shaped Stones | Waterfall, White Buffalo Woman, heart rock, crystal bioamplifier idea. | Tears = purification; rock = pineal crystal. | Nature = oracle. Lesson: Gifts (rock) = faith seeds; inspiration from love refines soul. |

| Chapter 9: City Lights and Stolen Dreams | Mall chaos, stolen letter, blank page. | Urban illusion (neon = false light); blank = void/enlightenment potential. | Betrayal = test of faith. Lesson: Material pursuits trap; messengers (Harold) guide back to purpose. |

| Chapter 10: Shattered Dreams and Silent Goodbyes | Hospital death, "Row Your Boat," bar despair. | Song = life as dream/reincarnation stream. | Death = transition. Lesson: Grief fuels creation; don't quit (soul's eternal game). |

| Chapter 11: Courtroom Tides | Lawsuit, package proof, victory. | Justice = balance (scales); time-stamp = divine timing. | Trials = soul tests. Lesson: Truth (heart rock) overcomes lies; past acts (Stacy's mail) save future. |

| Chapter 12: Pixels of Healing | Reef of Dreams game, healing tech. | Pixels = simulated realms (dream within dream); reef = neural/soul networks. | Technology = tool for enlightenment. Lesson: Turn loss into legacy (resurrection via creation). |

| Epilogue: Echoes of the White Buffalo | Waterfall return, reincarnated Stacy, "Mr. Mustard Seed." | Cycle complete (White Buffalo peace); seed recognized. | Full awakening. Lesson: Souls reconnect across lives; faith moves mountains (embryonic to eternal). |

This table serves as a "key" for rereading: Cross-reference symbols (e.g., rocks/crystals = pineal) and apply lessons (e.g., view inventions as alchemical soul work). It enhances the story's depth without spoiling the plot, encouraging meditation on themes like faith, reincarnation, and neuro-spiritual unity.